The Chrysanthemum Kimono

A parable of the power of beauty…
and a bit of thread

Elaine D.K. Hargrove

Elaine D.K. Hargrove

DEDICATION

Dedicated to all wise artists who work in thread and fiber, who know the power of both its beauty and importance in building culture...and even empires. Most especially to embroiderers Helen McCook, who believed I could do this, and Jen Goodwin, who loves cats.

The Chrysanthemum Kimono

There was once a Warrior who was young, but very strong and ambitious. He was the master of a large and prosperous estate, located at the top of a mountain. A magnificent home was located at the center of his land, large enough to embrace an inspiring courtyard, rooms enough for many wives, all their children and all their servants. Outside the house was a garden, bursting with flowers and acclaimed by all who knew of it. Beyond the garden lay acres and acres of famously fertile land. He was very wealthy indeed.

In his youth he took a beautiful woman for his Wife, the Daughter of another Warlord, thereby sharing and keeping the land and the power between them.

But as the Young Warrior grew older, he lusted after more power and more beautiful women. He took a Second Wife, just as beautiful as his First, and brought her into his home.

But where the Warrior's First Wife was merely beautiful, the Warrior's Second Wife was beautiful as well as well-educated. She could read and write all manners of things - history and fairy tales and poetry - even music. She could paint and draw; she did many things with books and paper and silk and parchment and ink and all forms of coloring medium. But there was more.

She was kind.

This made the Warrior's First Wife very jealous. She felt dull and plain next to the Second Wife, even though they were equally beautiful. But when guests would come and eat with their Warrior Husband, the Warrior's First Wife noticed the male guests paid more attention to the Warrior's Second Wife. Her speech was kind and her voice melodious. She had self-confidence but not arrogance. And she had an inner peace that made her face glow and her eyes shine.

One day, as their Warrior Husband bragged to others about some land he had conquered, the Warrior's First Wife overheard the Warrior's Second Wife talking to others about the property. It was clear the Warrior's Second Wife had somehow learned about this land and the things that could make it valuable to them; things like what kind of soil it had, and what crops could best be grown there to increase their wealth above which they already had. The conversation of the Warrior's Second Wife was wise and thoughtful; the conversation of their Warrior Husband harsh and cruel, for he only spoke of the battles he had fought, and the men he had killed. His thoughts were all about conquest; those of the Warrior's Second Wife dealt with blossoming and growth.

The Warrior's First Wife burned with jealousy for the attention her Warrior Husband paid the Warrior's Second Wife (although, in all honesty, he loved the First Wife more because he and she were so alike). So the First Wife went to her Warrior Husband and cruelly lied, saying, "Look, she belittles you when she speaks. It would be best you take away her books and her pens and her paper. Lock her away so she can't make trouble for you. You can still go to her if you like, for your pleasure. But lock her away before she brings shame on your reputation."

And so the Warrior's Second Wife was locked away in her own quarters, away from the rest of the household. There was a little hallway that served as an entrance, and then a bare second room where she slept and spent her days. The far wall opened up into a portion of the household garden, a space about the same size as her room. It had been beautifully landscaped with flowers and shrubs and a young tree; there was also a bit of sand she could arrange as she liked, but the garden was walled in on the three outside walls. All she could see above her was a bit of sky.

She sat in the empty room that was now her prison. Boredom filled her mouth and throat; she felt she would drown in it.

She had absolutely nothing to do.

For weeks, her routine consisted of getting up in the morning, sitting patiently while servants bathed and dressed her, fixed her hair and did her face. And then she sat in a corner of her room, on her mat, until the servants brought her her meals. She would eat, then return to her corner, arms bent at the elbows, her hands folded neatly in her sleeves, looking through the open door of her room out into the garden.

****

Occasionally, her Warrior Husband would call for his Second Wife to pleasure him. But all he craved was her body, not her mind. When he was done with her, he sent her back to her room. She returned to her corner, staring out into the garden, watching the days go from sun to rain, to cloud or fog or snow. When it was dark, she slept. Morning came, and her cycle began again.

One day, as the sun was ever so slightly changing its angle in the sky, it lit the floor across from her and she spotted an object lying there she had never noticed before. It was bright and shiny - thinner than a grain of rice but three times as long. Its shine seemed like it was singing cheerily to her. Intrigued, she unfolded her hands from inside her kimono, got to her feet and crossed to it.

It was a thin piece of wire, but incredibly rigid. One end was sharp; the other end dull, but with a tiny, oblong hole that seemed to wink merrily at her. It fit nicely between her thumb and her index and middle fingers. Perhaps it was some clothing or hair accessory left behind by the last inhabitant. She decided to show it to her Hairdresser, and tucked it into the hem of her sleeve.

****

The next morning she presented her Hairdresser with the little piece of wire, its little metal body still seeming so cheery to her. But her Hairdresser did not see its charms; instead the servant laughed as if it were only something extraordinarily common. "That, milady? You've never seen one before? It's a needle!"

"A needle? What is a needle?"

"It's used for sewing, milady."

"And what is sewing?"

The Warrior's Second Wife had never been taught to sew; her father had raised her to be a consort to a ruler. She had learned the crafts of leadership, such as reading and writing, studying history, philosophy, and diplomacy. But never sewing. In the household of her youth, sewing - even the fine embroidery of her clothes - had been done by servants. And so, for her, clothes and the art that decorated them seemed magically to come out of nowhere.

"What is sewing?" The Hairdresser echoed, aghast. She plucked the sleeve of the kimono of the Warrior's Second Wife. "*This* is sewing, milady."

"But that is fabric," the Warrior's Second Wife said.

"Indeed it is, milady, but it is sewing that makes the fabric flow across the body, rather than hang in shapeless folds from one's neck."

The Warrior's Second Wife had never thought of this. She stood, walked to the center of her room, lifted her arms and considered her kimono - how it draped from her shoulders to the floor; how it followed her torso yet allowed for her long, full sleeves. Of course. She could see it now. Fabric alone couldn't cover her body like this. Someone had engineered how it must be cut, then put together again in a meaningful way. She moved this way and that, marveling for the first time how the fabric that seemed to follow her frame and her every move like a mist, covering her at the same time allowing her great freedom of movement. It was a miracle!

And as she moved her arms, she noticed something else for the first time - there were flowers covering the sea green silk. She'd worn this kimono many times before, and had noticed the flowers before, and thought they were lovely, flowing over the silk as if they were floating in a pond. Before, that was as far as her thinking took her. But now, she turned back the sleeves of her kimono, touching the threads she found there, done so neatly the front carried seamlessly to the back. "And is this sewing, too?" she asked the Hairdresser.

"Yes, milady."

"But it looks so different."

"It's a different kind of sewing, milady."

"It is? What is it called?"

"Embroidery, milady."

The Warrior's Second Wife studied the flower on her sleeve for several moments, analyzing the colors and the lay of the stitches. The Hairdresser watched her, not daring to breathe. After a time, the Warrior's Second Wife walked to the part of her room overlooking the garden, holding up her sleeve as if comparing the flower on her sleeve to the flowers in the garden.

"Interesting," she finally murmured. "It is just as beautiful, but it will never wilt."

"No," the Hairdresser agreed. "Embroidery never will."

The Warrior's Second Wife returned to her corner, folding herself up into her usual seated position, looking out into the garden. But now she fingered the sleeve of her kimono thoughtfully, running her fingers over and over at the flower there, caressing it, noting how the differences in the stitches - raised or smooth or knobby - affected the texture; even the way the color attracted the light. Waiting to be dismissed, the Hairdresser could only watch her and wait.

"Hairdresser," the Warrior's Second Wife finally said, "is there someone you know who could teach me this embroidery?"

The Hairdresser nodded. "My sister, the Seamstress, has recently been apprenticed here in your very house, and she is already very good. I will ask her to teach you if you would like, milady."

But the Warrior's Second Wife remembered the cruelty of her husband. What if he denied her request to have the Seamstress teach her? Or worse yet, punished the young woman out of rage for her request of him? No, she had to be very wise, very sly in asking this.

She shook her head and waved the little Hairdresser away. "No. Not today, I'm afraid. But don't forget my request."

****

Two nights later, her Warrior Husband sent for her. The Warrior's Second Wife called the Hairdresser to help her make herself especially beautiful for him. "Do not get your hopes up," the Warrior's Second Wife warned the Hairdresser, "But tonight I will ask my husband if your sister may teach me embroidery." And together the Warrior's Second Wife and her Hairdresser worked to make her look more beautiful than she had ever looked before.

She entered her Warrior Husband's chambers as gracefully as if gliding on a frozen pond, her hair done to its best effect and her makeup flattering to her dark eyes and high cheekbones.

But he barely looked at her; in fact, he did not want her for pleasure at all. He simply wanted to announce:

"In three months' time I will take a New Bride. She is younger and prettier than you. I will still keep you as my Second Wife, but my New Bride will be my Favorite."

It was as if her Warrior Husband had taken a knife and cut her arm to the bone. She wanted to cry and run out of the room, but instead she thought quickly.

Composing her face into a smile, she bowed to her Warrior Husband. "Then I must congratulate my Master on this good news," she said.

He was surprised.   He had expected her to be jealous and angry, or hurt and tearful. But she was neither. She was gracious.

"And if it please my Master, perhaps he would grant his most Unworthy Second Wife a favor…"

Here it is, her Warrior Husband thought. She's pretending to be obedient to get something from me. He leaned back in his chair, smiling, certain he knew her strategy. "I will consider your request," he said, believing he never would, but that he would toy with her awhile. "What is it?"

"A plain kimono that I may embroider for your New Bride, if she will accept so lowly a gift from my Warrior Husband's Second Wife."

This was not what he expected. A cosmetic, perhaps, that his Second Wife would lace with some substance that would burn or discolor his New Bride's youthful skin. Or some sweet delicacy his Second Wife would taint so his New Bride would be tempted to eat it, fall sick, perhaps even die.

But a kimono?

He thought a moment. How could she harm his Beautiful New Bride with a kimono? What was behind his Second Wife's request? Lost in thought, he was silent for quite some time, until he realized the others in the room - servants, some of his officers and their ladies, visiting dignitaries from nearby regions - were watching him. He had to say something; he was losing face.

At last he asked, "What color?" T

he Warrior's Second Wife bowed graciously to him. "If it please my Lord, a gray kimono - the color of the sky just as the sun has begun to defeat the darkness."

He nodded, then gave her a wave with the back of his hand in a casual sign of dismissal, as if she mattered no more to him than one of his dogs. "Very well. Go away. You bore me."

She turned to go, but stopped once more and turned again. "One more thing, if it please my Lord... Some needles, just one or two... And a little thread?"

Her request would cost him but a pittance, and by now his mind had turned to some horses he was considering buying for his soldiers. "Yes, yes, whatever you want." And he waved her away again.

She turned to go, but stopped, seemed to think a moment before turning again, her brows curved in regret. But she had calculated this moment carefully, if quickly. "One last request, my Warrior Husband. I would like someone to teach me to do this needlework with great skill, to honor my Warrior Husband's Most Worthy New Bride. May I have a Seamstress to teach me?"

He was now annoyed. He wanted to be rid of her, to concentrate on his fantasies of his New Bride. He waved his Second Wife away. "Yes, yes. Do whatever you want. You have my consent."

She ran to the servants' quarters, her feet and her spirits lighter than they had been in many years.

****

The Seamstress began joining her every day. Until her Warrior Husband's New Bride's kimono arrived, they practiced stitches on scraps of cloth and drew patterns in the sand of the garden. But finally the kimono arrived, wrapped in a layer of silk. The Warrior's Second Wife lifted it from its folds. It was a beautiful pale blue gray, slightly paler at the shoulders than at the hem, as if the woman wearing it was rising from the darkness of the dawn just as the day does when it begins.

And suddenly the Warrior's Second Wife became afraid. What if, instead of creating something beautiful with this kimono, she utterly destroyed it? What if her lack of skill thoroughly undermined her good intentions?

She felt a light touch on her arm. It was the Seamstress. "I know what you're thinking," she told the Warrior's Second Wife. "You will not ruin it. I will be here. I will help you." She smiled. "Let's get to work."

They had three months before her Warrior Husband's New Bride arrived. First, they studied the kimono to decide how to embroider it for best effect; what design would meet the Warrior's Second Wife's skills with needle and thread, and what materials they had on hand. Stars, they decided, cascading over her shoulders and down the front, then all the way around the hem, looking as though they had been caught there as she traveled the distance from her home to theirs. The stitches could be simple, but if spaced with care, it could be quite striking.

The Seamstress and the Warrior's Second Wife spent hours together every day, each woman sewing her own embroidery project. The Warrior's Second Wife studied the Seamstress as she sewed for her Warrior Husband's First Wife and her three daughters, lovely little floral petals of all sizes and shapes, merrily punctuated by a butterfly or a dragonfly or an industrious little bee. Her skill dazzled the Warrior's Second Wife and made her despair of her own simple efforts. But wisely, she stuck to the simple, straight shapes of the stars, focusing instead on keeping her stitches even and developing her eye for color and subtle shading.

When the Star Kimono was finished, only a few days remained before her Warrior Husband's New Bride's arrival. The household was in a flurry of activity making ready. But the Warrior's Second Wife was excluded from it all. So she sat in her room, quiet and alone. To one side of her hung the Star Kimono, a crowning achievement of her first efforts;

to the other, her garden, vibrant with colors and textures that challenged her to take on a new project and raise her skill to yet a new level.

The day to greet her Warrior's New Bride finally arrived. The Warrior's New Bride, together with her family, came riding on horses, finally reaching the end of a long and dusty journey. The Warrior and his First Wife, many of his Soldiers and their Ladies, with many of the household servants, went out to greet them. They carried food and water and tea, cool wet cloths and many other things for The Travelers to refresh themselves.

The Warrior's Second Wife carried the Star Kimono, carefully wrapped in a layer of silk.

The people of her Warrior Husband's household merged with the people of his New Bride, like freshwater merging onto parched land, offering the people food and drink. But the Warrior's Second Wife walked confidently to her Warrior Husband's New Bride, sitting in a chair carried on two poles by servants. Her Warrior Husband's New Bride was behind a curtain, and her face behind a veil, but nevertheless, the Warrior's Second Wife could tell her Warrior Husband's New Bride was very pretty, but also rather plump. It made her smile.

With great dignity, the Warrior's Second Wife offered her gift in both hands, her head bowed. "If it please my Warrior Husband's New Bride…"

Her Warrior Husband's New Bride reached through the curtains of her chair and took the bundle in a quick, rather greedy motion. She pulled the package through the curtains and unwrapped it, then stopped. After a moment, she lifted her veil and studied the gift, stunned. She pulled back the curtains to speak to the Warrior's Second Wife, but at just that moment, the entire Entourage moved forward with a lurch, and the Warrior's Second Wife was left behind in the dust.

With great dignity, she slid one arm over the other and into the long flowing sleeves of her kimono. She bowed in the direction of her Warrior husband's New Bride.

13

"You are most welcome," she said to the hot, dusty air.

****

The Warrior's New Bride wore the Star Kimono to the Feast that night, a feast whose purpose was to welcome her to the new family; a Feast which was designed to impress her father and her other male relatives with the strength and wealth of her Warrior Husband, sealing the alliance between their families. But in reality, meant to intimidate the Warrior's New Bride's family a little.

The Warrior's Wives had all been ordered to come that night; to make their hair and their faces as beautiful as they could, and to wear their best kimonos, to show off the skills of the household seamstresses and embroiderers.

And so they gathered that evening with their Warrior Husband's guests in the garden, lit by two thousand lanterns with pastel silken shades, blowing gently in the evening breeze like a meadow full of flowers.

They all stood in clusters, eating or drinking, the men separated for the most part from the women, but occasionally the sparkle of a woman's headdress would glitter through the haze of men like stars against a midnight sky.

But as for the Warrior's Second Wife, she stood by herself, off to one side, near one of the gardens. During her solitary hours embroidering she had enjoyed sitting near the garden outside her rooms. Not only was the light better there, but she found comfort in the serenity and silence of the flowers and the birds. And inspiration.

She knew if her Warrior Husband found her here, so far away from his guests, he would reprimand her for removing herself from the others. But actually this was the perfect place, for in one or two steps, she could be out in the open, in the light, her introversion cast aside in a flash.

And finally the moment arrived - the moment their Warrior Husband's New Bride entered the room to be welcomed officially into her new household. She came to them from the top of the steps, the night sky behind her. As she walked down the steps towards them, she appeared to be stepping out of the sky, enveloping a bit of star-studded black velvet around her as she emerged from the constellations. Although she was a rather plump young woman, the design on the kimono elongated her, making her seem taller and thinner.

The effect was stunning. The Warrior Husband's New Bride knew the Star Kimono flattered her. She was beaming. Every eye was on her. She had never worn anything so simple, so elegant, and that so completely fit her style and her personality in this most perfect moment of her life.

"Where did she get the kimono?" the Warrior's Other Wives and many of the guests asked. The weave of the fabric, and the cut of the kimono made it clear; it was in the style of the region. It had to have come from somewhere very nearby.

As the Warrior's New Bride reached the bottom step, her Warrior Husband stepped forward to take her hand. She met him with a warm smile and he began to introduce her to his First Wife and her three daughters. But the Warrior's New Bride kept looking around the room, her eyes sweeping the faces. When she finally spotted the Warrior's Second Wife, she ran to her, her eyes sparkling. "I want to thank you!" she cried, even though she was still many steps away. She spun around in the kimono, looking like a galaxy of stars taking a turn in space.

It was then the Warrior's Second Wife fainted.

****

When she awoke, she was back in her own room again. One of the housemaids to her Warrior Husband and the Seamstress were holding her between them, helping her undress. As they eased her out of her kimono, the Housemaid giggled. "Aha! Now I see the problem." And she patted the Warrior's Second Wife's rounded belly, a swelling she hadn't noticed growing, so taken was she by the task of working on the Star

Kimono for her Warrior Husband's New Bride's Star Kimono.

She was pregnant.

****

She was happy to be pregnant, but not happy the baby's father was her Warrior Husband. In her girlhood dreams, she would have had children with a man who was gentle and kind. Yet perhaps this wouldn't be so bad. Her Warrior Husband left his First Wife to herself when it came to matters concerning the three girls he had sired by her. Maybe he would leave her and her child alone as well.

In fact, he did exactly that with his Second Wife . He never sent for her during the entire course of her pregnancy. Since her Warrior Husband's First Wife had had nothing but girls, why shouldn't she expect the same?

As the Warrior's Second Wife waited for her baby's arrival, she busied herself by making little embroidered coats with daisies; little embroidered coats with roses; little embroidered slippers with butterflies on the toes. She embroidered caps with ladybugs and bumblebees.

And every moment she embroidered her daughter's exquisite clothes, she thought of her, longed for her - the chubby thighs and the flushed little cheeks; dark merry eyes that sparked and twinkled with every toss of her perfectly-shaped head.

But as much as her mind spun visions of the little girl she would give birth to, she longed to hold the child in her arms now. Yet for as hard as she willed it, her baby would not arrive. There was only the servant girl - the daughter of her Hairdresser - who entered her suite of rooms every day. And so, although the Warrior's Second Wife was quite fond of her, and even fantasized of the things her own daughter would do while staring at the servant girl, the Warrior's Second Wife never took the her in her arms, never caressed her, never brushed her hair back from her forehead or kissed her.

Such demonstrations of affection would be unseemly between the child of a servant and the Second Wife of a mighty and important Warrior.

Yet, her longing for something to hold tightly against her chest grew; borne out of her pregnancy and driven by maternal hormones. She thought she would go mad if she didn't find something to cuddle - and soon.

And then one morning, like the answer to a prayer - there it was.

A mewing in her garden.

The Warrior's Second Wife stepped out of her room onto the stone path. She couldn't see it, but the high-pitched, frightened mewing was unmistakable - and ear-piercing. She walked towards the sound cautiously, quietly, afraid a sudden noise or movement might frighten it away.

And there she found it, crouched in some plants near the far wall of her portion of the garden. It was a Kitten - wet, cold, hungry, and incredibly small. She picked it up, cupping it in her hands. It was trembling, its eyes darting everywhere, never resting, seeing danger in anything that moved.

She turned it this way and that, examining it gently. It was mostly white, except for its tail, which wasn't white at all, but ring upon ring of riotous color - brown, black, orange, then brown again, now orange - from tip to base. One ear was white, the other a patch of orange overlaid with a patch of brown, cockeyed, as if she were wearing a hat at a rakish angle. On her left flank was a patch of pumpkin, as if she had brushed up against a newly-painted surface in the house somewhere. Her nose and the insides of her ears were pink, as were all but one of the leathery pads on her feet. That one was a rebellious black.

The Kitten's trembling had eased a little by now, and she finally looked the Warrior's Second Wife directly in the eye, a little defiantly, the Warrior's Second Wife thought. It made her smile, and she stroked the Kitten's cheek with her finger.

The Warrior's Second Wife heard a noise behind her and turned. It was the Hairdresser's Daughter, a basket in her hands with embroidery. When the Warrior's Second Wife turned, the girl saw the Kitten she held in her hands. The Girl dropped the basket and ran to her, her hands held out to take the Kitten. "Where did you find her?" the Girl asked, enchanted.

The Warrior's Second Wife pointed to the garden wall. "Just over there," she said. "I think it's hungry."

The Girl nuzzled the Kitten's face, then handed her back to the Warrior's Second Wife. "I know just the thing," the Girl said with a smile. "I'll be right back."

She returned a short time later with a tray and three small bowls. One of them was full of water; one of them with milk, and the third with some cooked, crumbled fish mixed with a little rice. The Girl set the tray on the floor, and the Warrior's Second Wife set the Kitten in front of the tray. With a fierce savagery in one so small, the Kitten attacked the rice and fish first, then the milk, and finally the water before touching her reflection in it with her paw. She moved more slowly after that, her belly full and her little mind drowsy. Smitten, the Warrior's Second Wife picked up the Kitten and set it on her lap. Comforted by the warmth of her body, the Kitten fell asleep, kneading her paws in her sleep.

****

The Warrior's Second Wife became obsessed with the Kitten, even as she realized her love for it probably stemmed from the often unbearable swings of emotions she experienced due to her Daughter growing within her. Unable to cuddle her Unborn Daughter, the

Warrior's Second Wife instead cuddled the Kitten. For the most part, the Kitten didn't seem to mind. But other times, the Kitten wanted to play, and so, in the interest of the Kitten's physical and mental health, the Warrior's Second Wife amused them both with a length of string or an empty bobbin.

Every evening, the Kitten disappeared back into her garden. The Warrior's Second Wife would sometimes walk in the garden as darkness turned the day into evening, gently pushing away a leaf here or there, hoping to find the Kitten's hiding place. But she never did find it, and was forced to conclude the Kitten disappeared into the night further away than she would like to imagine. Thankfully, every morning, the Kitten returned.

****

Then, one morning, the Kitten didn't come back.

The Hairdresser's Daughter came to the quarters of the Warrior's Second Wife with her breakfast, and found the Warrior's Second Wife standing in the doorway of her portion of the garden, her face darkened with fear and concern. Her pregnancy was coming to an end; even through the layers of her kimono, the Hairdresser's Daughter could see the baby moving, roiling within its mother's belly impatiently. And for a moment, the Hairdresser's Daughter thought her mistress might be in labor.

But she wasn't. Her distress was due to the disappearance of the Kitten. Together, the Warrior's Second Wife and the Hairdresser's Daughter searched the garden, looking for any flash of orange and white fur among the grasses, leaves and flowers. But nothing. It was only with great difficulty that the Hairdresser's Daughter managed to drag the Warrior's Second Wife to her breakfast and tried to explain how it is often the way of cats to disappear for a few days, then come home again.

But the Warrior's Second Wife barely listened to her and instead stared out into the rain, chewing and swallowing food to sustain her baby, but barely giving a thought to the way it tasted in her mouth.

The Kitten remained missing another day, then another, and finally was missing a week. The Warrior's Second Wife fought from letting her emotions get the best of her, for the sake of upsetting her baby. No one ever saw or heard her cry. But her face remained dark; brown circles developed under her eyes, and her shoulders stooped under her beautiful kimono. Little imagination was needed to see the darkness surrounding her.

She awoke in the middle of the night, in the dark silence, alone. She could hear a low moaning in the distance, in her half-awake state, she thought it might be the kitten, come home. She sat up with a struggle, still fighting sleep, and realized the cries were her own and that she was just entering labor.

She sat in the darkness, in her damp nightclothes on her damp bamboo mattress, panting and staring into the darkness in front of her face, feeling as if she were staring into death. Women sometimes didn't survive childbirth, she thought. Why should she? No one was near her, not her mother, or her sister, or any other relative; not her husband; none of his other wives had seemed to take a liking to her; even the servants had abandoned her.

She put her face in her hands and cried.

But only a moment later, the door of her bedroom slid open and the Seamstress and her mother, who was one of the women who worked in the garden, entered. The Seamstress carried a number of towels over her arm; the Gardner carried a bowl of hot water.

"We heard you crying," the Seamstress said. "I thought maybe it was time for your baby to come. I called my mother to help."

Lanterns were quickly lit and the Seamstress's mother, a small, fine-boned woman with dark, merry eyes but a serious mouth, set to examining her. A moment later, she lifted her head and smiled at the

Warrior's Second Wife, a kind and happy smile. The Warrior's Second Wife was grateful for her kindness, but wondered how happy she would really be if she fully understood her situation. "Everything is going to be fine," the woman said. "The baby won't be much longer now."

But "much longer now" to the Seamstress's Mother and to the Warrior's Second Wife were two very different things. Night passed into morning; morning into noon of the hottest day in recent memory. The Warrior's Second Wife grew dull-witted from the pain and the stress of the baby on her body. She sweated through her thin cotton robe, squeezing the hand of the Seamstress's mother. Several times the face of her Warrior Husband floated before her, leering at her with a mixture of interest and delight. "Is it here yet?" he asked. When answered in the negative, he would grunt and leave the room.

The Seamstress and her mother soaked the clothes of the Warrior's Second Wife in cool water; they put a cup of cool water to her lips. The afternoon faded into twilight and she was hungry and oh, so tired. She wanted to give up and sleep, to let the baby do as it wished; even if that meant killing her. But the Seamstress's Mother kept telling her to push, kept bringing water to her lips, kept bathing her with cool cloths.

And finally, just as the last of the birds in the garden were finishing the last of their songs for the day, the baby came.

It was not a Girl.

It was a Boy.

As the Warrior's Second Wife waited for the Seamstress's Mother to clean up the child before handling him to her, she thought with regret of the beautiful clothing she had embroidered for the baby - the rosebud slippers, the goldfinch kimono, the pink kimono with the pretty little hummingbirds - all too delicate for the rough-and-tumble Warrior's Son her baby would undoubtedly grow up to be.

But the moment the Seamstress's Mother placed her son in her arms, all those thoughts fled from her like a roomful of cockroaches when a bright lantern is lit. She held the baby to her breast, marveling at his perfect but oh-so-tiny fingernails and nose, all the while noticing how wrinkled and purple he was, especially in those places where he had pressed against her pelvis as he had made his way out of her womb. She had heard the saying, "A face only a mother could love," and now she knew for herself how it could be so.

She was smitten.

But the Warrior's Second Wife, because she had never imagined herself giving birth to anything but a girl, had not considered the effect a Son would have on her Warrior Husband. When he was told he had a Son - after having three daughters from his First Wife - he ran to her room, grabbing the baby from her arms and unceremoniously digging through the baby's swaddling until he saw the truth of the child's gender for himself. He raised the child over his head, bellowing for joy, then ran from her quarters.

The Warrior's Second Wife would have followed him, but the Seamstress and her Mother held her back, reminding her she had just given birth and needed to rest. She sank back against the pillows, overcome by exhaustion and raging hormones, and gave herself over to tears.

Her Warrior Husband ran out into the grounds at the front of his great house, where all his soldiers and all their sons, some of them as young as three years old, stood waiting to hear the news. Standing on the top stair of his house, so everyone had a clear view, the Warrior unwrapped his Son, exposing him for all to see. "I have a Son!" he cried, the baby's swaddling curling down around his arms and onto the ground. "It's a Boy!"

And all his soldiers and all their sons cheered. It was a wonderful feeling, knowing he finally had a Son he could train in the art of warfare, a son to carry on his name, to be his legacy, to pray to him and for him in death.

He lowered the baby and studied its face a moment, his elation gradually deflating. He was suddenly aware of the fact that this creature was merely hours old; that it was helpless and far from being a warrior. Twisting the trailing swaddling around one arm so he wouldn't step on it and fall, he turned and went back into the house.

****

The Warrior entered the room of his Second Wife. She was sitting up and weeping, despite the efforts of the Seamstress and her Mother to have her rest, her face completely shattered in fear and despair. For a moment, the Warrior was overwhelmed by the miracle she had presented him and how much her labor had cost her. "I will give you anything you want," he promised her with all his heart.

The Warrior's Second Wife held out to hands to him, hands that reached out not from her shoulders, but from the ache in her chest. "Give me my Son," she begged.

For a moment, he clearly saw how he had pained her, and he quickly complied, laying the baby in her outstretched arms. Her relief was released in a loud hiccup, and she pressed the baby against her chest, wrapping him snugly in his swaddling again.

The Warrior watched her a moment, ashamed. "I mean it," he finally said. "You have honored me with a great gift. What can I give you in return?"

But the Warrior's Second Wife was already so wounded by his earlier treatment of her; the way he had ignored her, favoring his other, younger wives over her. And now, even though she had presented him with a Son, she knew he would soon go back to forgetting about her; he had learned he was already negotiating a fifth marriage - or was it his sixth? - for another warrior's daughter in order to forge a new alliance.

She said nothing to answer his question.

He looked around her room, plain and clean and stark. There

were no clues here, nothing that gave him any insight into her heart's desire.

And then his eye fell on a simple basket on a shelf. He walked to it, tipping it forward so he could see what it contained. He found a magnificent tangle of thread, bursting and flashing in pastel and jewel tones, the trimmings left from the stunning Star Kimono his Second Wife had given his New Bride.

He turned to her.

"I will give you a kimono and all the thread you will need to make your most magnificent kimono ever," he promised.

And with this, his conscience was appeased. He turned and left the room.

****

But the Warrior's Second Wife soon forgot his promise to her; he so rarely followed through on anything he said. Instead, she became absorbed in raising her Son. But much to her surprise, one day the Seamstress came to her, carrying a large package wrapped in plain muslin.

Inside was a kimono in the finest silk, dyed a rich midnight blue. A few days later, another package arrived, this one bursting open in a firework's display of bright and festive colors, more threads than she could use in a lifetime.

And that same day, the Kitten returned. Only she was no longer a Kitten, she was a full-grown Cat. And with her were six kittens, looking so much like their mother, it was as if they were cut from the same cloth.

And ironically, all of them were girls.

****

It took her a long time to decide what she could create with the midnight blue kimono. She was afraid of beginning a work on it that would be unworthy of its value. So every week, she took it from its shelf, unwrapped it from its muslin, unfolded it and admired it, turning it over and over in her hands, examining the front, the back, the full and flowing sleeves, the hem. Some days she even tried it on. But it always ended the same, folding the kimono back, neatly arranged in a slightly different way than before so it wouldn't crease into the same folds time and again, and slipped it back into its muslin case.

More frequently, she took out the collection of threads and looked at them - the silvers and golds, the brilliant reds, greens and blues, the soft yellows and pinks. Some of the colors suggested fruits to her, like peaches or lemons; others reminded her of jewels, like emeralds or sapphires; others suggested treasures of the sea, like shimmering fish scales or pastel sea glass washed up on the shore.

The kimono and the threads delighted her, but they did not speak to her; they did not tell her what they were destined to become. And so she would sigh and line the shanks of thread up neatly again, organized from red to purple like a rainbow, and put them away again with their quiet but twinkling needles.

Meanwhile, her Son grew. He learned to roll over, then to crawl; then to walk with halting, clumsy steps. His youthful awkwardness seemed not to matter to him at all. He didn't care if he looked clumsy or silly or undignified. He was walking; he was walking his way, and when he was good and ready, he would get better at it. His main motivation for movement was going after the little white and orange Cat and her Kittens, but the Warrior's Second Wife did her best to teach him to play with the little Cat Family and not hurt them; to be gentle and kind.

And so, even still a babe, he continued to chase after the Cats, but stopped himself from hurting them. He'd read their feline moods and play with them when they felt energetic, or let them go if they had had enough.

This pleased the Warrior's Second Wife; she thought it showed wisdom and discernment and self-control; qualities she did not see in her Warrior Husband. His only thoughts were to be a great leader. He believed power could only be found in fighting. But his Second Wife, for all the reading she had done as a girl, believed true power was found in self-discipline, power over self, and wisdom.

The way a true emperor would be, she suddenly realized one day. An emperor who would wield great power, but who was fair and wise and kind to his subjects.

And her Son reminded her of a little emperor, the way he made everything in the world seem to belong to him in an amusing and benign way, from his food to his clothes to the Cats to his mother's room and her piece of the garden.

And suddenly, one day, she realized what she must embroider on the beautiful midnight blue kimono.

She would embroider her kimono with Chrysanthemums - the symbol of the emperor himself.

Perhaps it was too bold of her, to imagine herself at a level to wear the symbol of the emperor. But it was what the blue of the kimono was calling out for; begging her to adorn it with. She could see it in her mind's eye as surely as if it were already embroidered on the silk - chrysanthemums like the explosions of fireworks in full bloom, a bouquet of hot whites and yellows and glowing golds, hot as the heat of a fire and yet controlled and serene.

She spent a week designing it. There would be a large chrysanthemum on the back, another on the front, but continued over the two sides of the front so that they evenly came together when the kimono was tied. There would be one smaller chrysanthemum on the right sleeve, and two on the left that were slightly smaller still; one above and slightly to the side of the other, the bottom one seeming to fall off the edge of the sleeve.

She began sewing as soon as the design was finished. She let the design flow from her needle as it wished. Some days it seemed to spin out from her fingers like the glistening web of a frantic spider; other times, the design seemed to beg her to stop and consider where it would most naturally go next.

She didn't fight either extreme, or anything in the middle. She let it grow as it wished, the way her Son did, or the Kittens.

Her Son and the Kittens became great friends. She loved to watch them play together, sometimes gentle, sometimes rough-and-tumble. They were each regal and majestic in their own way, and the way they complimented and contrasted against one another was magical.

Her Warrior Husband came to visit now and again to see how his Son was doing. But typically he watched his Son a moment, made an approving grunt, and then left.

The Warrior's Second Wife would respectfully put down her sewing when he arrived, tucking it back in its basket on a shelf if she had enough warning. It somehow seemed too personal, too sacred, for her Warrior Husband's uncultivated eye.

Or perhaps she was embarrassed for him to see her working on the Emperor's emblem, the chrysanthemum. Maybe she was making herself more than she ought to be, wrapping herself in the sign of the Emperor.

Her Warrior Husband never saw the kimono, or if he did, he never mentioned it.

Her Warrior Husband was taking a greater interest in their Son as he grew. Had he learned to crawl? Her Warrior Husband paid a visit. A new tooth? Her Warrior Husband paid a visit. Had he learned to dress himself? Her Warrior Husband paid a visit.

As his visits increased, so did the interest of her Warrior Husband's Other Wives. They became jealous of the time their Warrior Husband spent on his Son when they wanted attention from him for their

Daughters as well. Whenever their Warrior Husband went to the rooms of his Second Wife, the other Wives would gather in the corridor to watch from the windows outside her room and tittered throughout his visit with his Second Wife.

One day, one of them asked, as their Warrior Husband left the room after his visit, "Why couldn't we let all the Children play together?" Of course, the truth of the matter was that she hoped that their Warrior Husband would visit during the Children's playtime and give attention to their Daughters as well. But the Warrior's Second Wife did not notice the deception, she merely assumed that being with other Children would be good for her son, and wondered if she had perhaps been too protective of him.

The Warrior's Second Wife agreed.

And so, after that, they began to meet in the large common courtyard of the house. The Six Wives of their Warrior Husband (was it really Six Wives already, the Warrior's Second Wife wondered?) were gathered there with their Daughters. The children playing in the courtyard in front of their mothers while the women sat to one side, playing a variety of women's games and gossiping.

Meanwhile, their children played their own games. These were sometimes games their mothers organized for them (although when the Warrior's Second Wife suggested games for the children, her suggestions were dismissed before she had barely even mentioned them). Other times the children organized their own games, or sometimes played alone.

The Warrior's Second Wife soon noticed with quiet amusement that it was the children of the most dominant of Her Warrior Husband's Wives that issued the most viable of the orders to the other children. But in time, her Son began to dominate even playing out battles from the history lessons she taught him, making his sisters line up and march like soldiers, even making the older girls get down on their hands and knees and pretend to be horses that the younger girls would ride.

As their children played, the Warrior's Second Wife sat by herself and embroidered quietly. For many weeks the other Wives paid her little attention, but as the chrysanthemums on her kimono grew, the brilliance of the colors drew them as if a moth to a flame.

"What are you making?" one of them finally asked her, her curiosity getting the better of her. It was clear none of them liked her. She wasn't sure if it was because she had produced a Son when the rest of them had only had daughters, or whether they resented her for keeping so much to herself. But she was determined to be pleasant, to keep peace in her Warrior Husband's household.

And so, in an act she would come to later regret, she halted her needle and slid it into the fabric for safekeeping. She lifted her kimono by the shoulders, showing the kimono's front, then its back to the rest of the Warrior's Wives.

Her work was stunning.

Jealousy lit up in their hearts like the flame of the swordsmith, hot and red and biting. "Oh!" one of the other Wives quickly said. "May I have it when you're done?"

The eyes of all the other Wives flashed in rage and greed. Each of them wanted the Chrysanthemum Kimono equally as badly, and were furious that each of them were not the wife who had spoken first.

Their rage frightened the Warrior's Second Wife. She quickly dropped the kimono in her lap, wadding it into a ball she knew would crumple her work, but at the moment, she didn't care; she just wanted it hidden from the greedy eyes of the other Wives. She wanted to cry. No one had complimented her; she could sense each of the other Warrior Wives' hands reaching out, trying to grab her kimono away from her. There was no kindness toward her or admiration for her skill in their reaction.

Clutching her kimono tightly in one hand, she stood and reached out for her Son with the other. "Son," she called softly.

He left the other Children and went to her. She took his hand and returned with him to their room.

****

The Warrior's Second Wife continued to meet with their Warrior Husband's Other Wives; and her Son continued to play with his Sisters. But their sessions were short, and the Warrior's Second Wife no longer brought her Chrysanthemum Kimono to embroider. She now sat to the side of the others, her hands folded quietly in her lap, tortured by their silence.

However, in an effort to calm the jealousy of their Warrior Husband's Other Wives, she did bring their daughters the many things she had embroidered for her Son - the slippers, the robes, the sashes and the belts. One by one, she handed them all out to the girls, carefully selecting which daughter should get which item, based on the girl's personal interest or coloring, and doing her best to be fair. After several weeks, everything she had embroidered for her expected daughter was gone.

She would see the little girls wearing her creations as they gathered for their playtime in the courtyard. Slippers became scuffed by the gravel; belts and sashes tattered with horseplay; hats became soggy and sank in the pond. It broke her heart to see all her hard work cared for so heartlessly, but she reminded herself they had been a gift to them, and now she had no say as to what would become of them.

Meanwhile, the Warrior's Other Wives pestered her for a glimpse of her Chrysanthemum Kimono.

"How is it coming?" one wife asked.

"Why don't you bring it to the courtyard to stitch?" another asked.

"You must be nearly finished with it," another said. "Surely you wouldn't want to hide something so beautiful…"

The Warrior's Second Wife looked at her. Her words were sweet, but they had passed through lips pulled back in a leer. It made her feel extremely ill at ease. She stood and held out her hand to her Son.

"Son," she said.

The Boy came to her and they returned to their quarters.

****

She continued embroidering the Chrysanthemum Kimono in her room, hoping she could hide her work there, and do it quickly, serenely, with just her Son and the white and orange Cat at her feet.

But it only took the others a few days to realize where she had gone and what she was doing.

They gathered at the open spaces between her room and the hallway that ran alongside it, not just pressing through the openings, but sticking their heads and arms through, even lifting their Daughters up to stand on the ledges to catch a glimpse of her working.

"When will it be finished?" one of the Warrior's Other Wives asked her.

The question caught her off-guard. She lifted the kimono from her lap and studied it. "Another week, I suppose."

A greedy hand suddenly flew at her through one of the open partitions. "I want it!" one of the Warrior's Other Wives cried out. The Warrior's Second Wife could not see her face, it was lost in one of the many dark shadows that seemed to symbolize the living, moving, shifting evil that resided in the house.

"No!" the Warrior's Second Wife cried, wrenching the Kimono away from them and to safety. She stood and backed away from the open wall to the far wall of her room, away from the wall of grabbing arms and glistening, greedy eyes, all coveting her work, this Kimono that bore a piece of her heart in every thread. "Please go away! Leave me alone!"

She had backed as far away from them as she could. She was pressed against the far wall, weeping, her Son clutching her legs, the cat hidden underneath a chest, its eyes glowing out at them like two bright, fiery copper coins.

The commotion summoned the Seamstress and she ran down the hall from the kitchen as quickly as she could, until she ran into the cluster of Warrior Wives clogging the hall. She pushed her way through them all until she stood at the entrance of the room of the Warrior's Second Wife. For a moment, she took in the scene: the pale Warrior's Second Wife, clutching her half-finished Kimono to her chest with one hand, the other hand protectively on her Son's head as he clung to her knees; the frightened Cat under the chest with her Kittens. On the other side of the room, waiting in the shadows, were the Warrior's Other Wives, their faces red with greed and desire.

She was just a Seamstress; what could she do? How could she stand up to so many of her Mistresses in one moment? Surely she would be removed from her post and thrown out into the street - and that would be a good outcome. She had known some seamstresses who would have been beheaded for less.

Yet, she knew the right thing needed to be done, and she had to get it right. She made herself as tall as she possibly could, and framed her words as if her life depended on it. "My most Worshipful Ladies," she said in a respectful yet horrified tone, "surely you can all understand it is a grievous state of events to upset your Warrior Husband's Only Heir, and His Mother as well? Please let them both have some rest, and I will make you all a sumptuous dessert later this evening - the most fanciful you have ever seen!"

They all turned and stared at her. The Seamstress swallowed. She had to tempt them away.

"It's a recipe I learned straight from the Emperor's kitchen!"

That caught their attention. They were murmuring now, murmuring carried lightly on a wave of happy anticipation and wonder, not the greed of a moment ago.

The Seamstress looked over her shoulder at the Warrior's Second Wife and gave her a smile of reassurance. The Warrior's Second Wife relaxed a little and smiled back at her faintly, still too worried to give her a full smile. The Seamstress turned to the Warrior's Other Wives again. "And, as a special treat, I will even invite you into the kitchen to watch me prepare it if you wish!"

"Now?" one of them asked, her voice squeaking in excitement.

"Of course now!" the Seamstress cried.

And suddenly the crowd of them dispersed, running down the hall to the kitchen, each one jostling for the place ahead. In the matter of a moment, the hallway was cleared.

The Warrior's Second Wife finally let out the breath she had been holding in a whoosh. "Thank you," she said to the Seamstress.

****

After that, the Warrior's Other Wives never again tried to reach through the partitions separating her room from the hall. However, that didn't stop them from standing at the partitions, staring at her while she worked.

And whenever the Warrior's Second Wife took her Son out to play in the courtyard with his Sisters, the other Warrior Wives gathered around her, not touching her but nevertheless surrounding her, creating a cage around her with their bodies. "Is it finished?" "Will you give it to me when you're done?" "No! Give it to me!" "No! To me!" they would cry.

The Warrior's Second Wife found herself moving from being fearful of them, then to amused. There was no way anyone but she would wear the Chrysanthemum Kimono when it was finished. She merely kept quiet, saying not a word as they called after her, as she walked with her Son to the courtyard and back again.

The frustration of the Warrior's Other Wives began to mount. Soon they began offering her their treasures - sweets, jewels, precious gifts they'd been given by their Warrior Husband. But the Warrior's Second Wife would have none of it.

And then one evening, she was sitting on the floor of her room, working on the Chrysanthemum Kimono, nearly finished with it. The kimono was pooled in her lap, spilling over her thighs to her right.

The Warrior's Other Wives were there, on the other side of the partition between her room and the hallway, hidden in the shadows. But she could hear them whispering, hatching plots to get the kimono away from her.

The Cat entered her room from the garden, having finished her evening rounds, hunting for mice. She was alone now, her children old enough to live on their own. The Cat walked in front of the Warrior's Second Wife, long enough to get her ears scratched. And then the Cat continued on, turning in front of the Warrior's Second Wife, and walked onto the kimono.

The Warrior's Other Wives all gasped and stepped forward, their faces pale. Many of them even dared to put their faces through the partition.

The Cat began to bathe, taking long, luxurious passes across her fur with her tongue.

The Warrior's Second Wife smiled to herself, but kept her head bent over her work so the others couldn't see her smile.

"Look," one of the Warrior's Other Wives said, pointing through the partition. "The Cat is on the Kimono!"

"So she is," the Warrior's Second Wife said, petting the cat. The Cat rolled over contentedly, showing her belly. The Warrior's Second Wife rubbed her. Fur floated up from the Cat, catching the light of the setting sun. It hung in the air a moment, then floated down to settle on the exquisite embroidery.

"Do something!" one of the Warrior Other Wives pleaded. "That cat will ruin the kimono if you don't move her off!"

But by now the Cat had finished her bath and curled up to go to sleep. The Warrior's Second Wife stroked the Cat's back as she dozed. "No," she said quietly. "I'll let her stay." And the Warrior's Second Wife returned to her work, contentedly stitching for several moments while the Warrior's Other Wives squirmed and twisted and grumbled out in the hallway.

Her Son, meanwhile, had been in the other room while his Nurse had been giving him a bath before bed. Her Son ran to his Mother, his arms out to her for a hug, still pink from his bath, his hair still wet. The Warrior's Second Wife dropped her work and caught him in her arms, hugging him tightly. He smelled of clean clothes and soap, grassy and lemony and fresh.

He had spent longer than usual playing outside that day, and it was summer. He had been tired at dinner and had barely been able to stay awake to eat. Now, after his bath, he was relaxed and so dozy, he almost seemed a little drunk. He sank into her, his head on her shoulder.

She had to tuck him in for the night. He was getting big. He weighed so much her legs were falling asleep where he pressed against her; so was her arm under his head. And yet the Cat was lying on the Kimono! She had to move, yet in seemingly every way imaginable, she was pinned down.

And then the solution came to her - absolutely delicious in its elegance and utter defiance.

She reached into her sewing box with her free hand and cut through the sleeve of the Chrysanthemum Kimono, leaving the cat undisturbed. She wrapped the rest of the Kimono around her Son and carried him to his own sleeping mat in the corner, pulling the Kimono away from him as she wrapped him in his own bedclothes.

When she walked back to her sewing basket and the Cat still sleeping on the kimono piece she had cut away, she realized only one or two of her Warrior Husband's Other Wives were still there; the others had walked away, angry and discouraged. The Warrior's Second Wife sat down beside the Cat, straightened her work, found where she had left off and continued stitching.

"How can you do that?" one of her Warrior Husband's Other Wives cried.

The Warrior's Second Wife lifted her head from her work. "Do what?

"Just continue on like that! You've cut the sleeve off it! It's ruined now! Why keep working on it?"

The Warrior's Second Wife lifted the Kimono and studied it a moment. "But the embroidery is just as beautiful as before, isn't it?"

"But it's missing its sleeve!" the Other Wife cried, exasperated.

The Warrior's Second Wife innocently continued her performance, looking at the sleeve under the Cat. "And the embroidery there is also just as beautiful. What's the problem?"

The Warrior's Other Wife threw up her hands in despair and walked away. The Warrior's Second Wife smiled and bent her head over her work again. Well, that was, apparently, that. The Chrysanthemum Kimono was ruined. The Warrior's Other Wives were no longer interested in it, or her. Life could be peaceful again.

Problem solved.

****

When she awoke the next morning, the sleeve was still lying on the floor where she had left it. The Cat had played with in during the night, rolling in it and doing other rough and tumble play, so now it was wrinkled and even a little frayed along the cut edge.

Feelings of faint remorse rose up in her, but they were not strong, and she managed to stuff them down again fairly quickly. She folded up the sleeve neatly and put it in the bottom of her sewing basket.

****

But things did not remain as peaceful as she might have liked. A few days later - after staying away from her for several weeks, her Warrior Husband came to her. His face was stern; he was clearly displeased with her. "I understand you have been causing trouble with my other wives," he told her.

She stared at him a moment, wondering if she dared to say it was the other way around - they were causing trouble for her. But she decided against it. So she stood meekly before him, her hands folded at her waist, her eyes cast down.

Their Son sat on the floor, not far away from them, playing a game with a ball. Her Warrior Husband looked at the boy. It was a quiet game he was playing, and gentle. The ball was multi-colored and when it rolled, it created a colorful effect on its surface. The boy rolled the ball back and forth, watching it dreamily, fascinated by the patterns it made.

"What's he doing?" her Warrior Husband asked, annoyed.

The Warrior's Second Wife knew her Son had just had his lunch, and now it was time for his nap. He was sleepy, and the ball was hypnotizing him. But she knew that no matter what she said, her Warrior Husband would belittle her for it.

37

And she knew what was coming.

And the pain would be great. She closed her eyes against what she knew was coming, but knew she was powerless against it.

Her Warrior Husband walked away from her and over to their Son. He bent down and picked up the ball. His Son looked up at him, as if surprised that his father had taken the ball away. His father held the ball out to the boy. "Do you really want this?" he asked him.

The boy nodded and held his hands out for the ball. "Yes, please," he said.

But his Warrior Father snatched it away, flinging the ball out of the room, into the garden and over the wall. "No!" he roared, thrusting his face into his Son's. "Balls are a girl's toy! Your Sisters play with balls! You are a boy! Boys play with sticks and horses!"

Her Warrior Husband spun back to his Second Wife. "It's your fault. You're raising him soft!"

She began to cry. "No, my Lord, no…"

"He will be a Warrior, like his father."

"Of course, my Lord."

"But he'll never grow into a Warrior the way you're raising him!"

"I will do better," she sobbed. "Let me try again."

But this was a stupid argument. It was the custom, in their country, that Warrior's Sons were taken from their mothers at the age of six to train with other boys to be warriors. And her son was five. A little early, perhaps, but not unheard of.

"I will be back for him in the morning," her Warrior Husband said.

He turned on his heel with a soldier's precision, and was out of

38

her room as swiftly and as boldly as a sword master cutting off the head of his enemy.

The Warrior's Second Wife was in shock. She turned to look at her Son, fearful he might already somehow be gone. But he stood there, off to the side of the room, right where he had been standing before, as tall and as straight as he could, the only thing betraying him were the tears in his eyes.

"Am I going away?" he asked her, quietly, incredulously.

She crossed the room to him quickly, putting her arm around his straight, brave, fragile shoulders, doing her best to suck in her own tears, forcing her face to crack into what she prayed might look like a smile. "Yes, my Son," she said, hugging him. "You have spent many, many months of your youth with me. Now it is time to be with your Father and learn to be a soldier."

He looked at her, his delicate eyebrows raised over his nose, his expression one of curiosity. "Will I learn to fight with a sword?"

"Yes, my love."

"Will I learn to ride a horse?"

"Of course."

He wrenched himself out of her arms, a pretend sword in his hand, the other rakishly on one hip, slaying imaginary enemies to his left and to his right. "Take that!" he cried. "And that! And that!"

In a matter of moments, his enemies all lay dead at his feet.

The Warrior's Second Wife clapped merrily for him, her eyes full of tears.

He was so incredibly clever.

****

That night she bathed him herself, sliding her hands over this little body that had grown inside of her such an incredibly short time before. He paid little attention to her, playing with the boats in his bath, sinking them and then pulling them up to the surface again, only to sink them in another mighty battle a moment later.

She pulled him out of his bath and dried him. As the cool evening enveloped him, he grew drowsy, sinking against her in a light sleep. She dressed him for bed and carried him to his sleeping mat. He fell asleep immediately and she laid next to him, twirling his hair around her finger, her head tilted so her tears wouldn't fall on his face. She never closed her eyes that night; she just stared into the darkness, drinking him in her all her senses - hearing him breathe, the smell of his hair, the touch of his youthful skin.

But the taste in her mouth was that of her own tears.

And the Cat, as if sensing she needed the comfort, came up behind her and curled up against the small of her back.

****

The next day, the Warrior's Second Wife rose early. For several moments, she watched her Son sleeping, the soft lavender light of dawn gracing his face. But she knew she had things to do. She left his side and quietly bathed, then dressed herself in the Chrysanthemum Kimono with the missing sleeve. By the time she was finished, her Son had awakened, and the Seamstress had arrived with the tray with their breakfast.

They quietly ate, and then the Warrior's Second Wife dressed her Son. As she did, she took the sleeve she had cut from the Chrysanthemum Kimono and wrapped it around his waist, under his clothing. "So you can remember me," she said, trying not to cry.

Her Son looked at her, still a little sleepy. He did not understand the gravity of the situation. He nodded, but she knew he only vaguely understood.

Time was flying by. He would be taken from her soon. She pondered other moments in her life, times she had been frightened or angry or confused - and how those moments had hung in the air forever as they happened, like glimpses of the eternal. Why couldn't time this morning last forever like that?

And then she heard it - the sounds of heavy footsteps coming down her corridor. It was her Warrior Husband with some of his soldiers, coming to take her Son away.

"Stand," she told her Son.

They stood together, the Boy in front of her, when her Warrior Husband entered the room, four of his men behind him. As if this were some sort of ceremony - and the Warrior's Second Wife supposed it was as they were all dressed in full armor and helmets - her Warrior Husband gave a slight nod, and the four soldiers came around from behind him. Two of them took her Son's shoulders and firmly pushed him towards the door. The other two took their places behind him as if to prevent his turning back; her Son walked between the four men. They went back down the corridor, her Warrior Husband following them. After a moment, the Warrior's Second Wife followed behind.

The seven of them - her Son boxed in by the four big soldiers, followed by his Warrior Father, then, a few steps behind, the Warrior's Second Wife - walked through the house and toward the formal courtyard. When they reached the top of the stairs, the men continued down the other side, into the courtyard and out the gate toward the outer edges of the estate to the area her Warrior Husband's soldiers trained and lived.

But the Warrior's Second Wife stood tall and erect and proud at the top of the stairs, a splendid figure in her dark Kimono lit by its fiery chrysanthemums, one sleeve shockingly removed, almost as jarring as if her whole arm were missing.

But despite her loss, she stood, her hands serenely folded at her waist, the chrysanthemums bursting from her kimono as if she was holding fireworks in her hands against a dark night sky.

Her young Son looked back only once for a final glimpse of her, and the sight of her standing there, light radiating from her, burned into his eyes like a goddess in a dream, though time would erase the moment's significance.

****

As for the Warrior's Second Wife, she stood at the top of the stairs for many hours after her Son disappeared past the household gates.

For a short time after her Son and the soldiers had left, other members of the household stood and watched her; so did many of the peasants who worked the estate fields. But when the dust raised by her Son, her Warrior Husband, and the soldiers accompanying them had settled, they all went about their business - doing their chores, scurrying here and there, chasing after their children.

Inside the close walls of her Warrior Husband's intimate household, it took a little longer for things to return to normal. The others, in their own ways, paid homage to the Warrior's Only Son through their silence, then stood motionless a little longer out of respect for his Mother.

But finally, they too, began to move again, to return to doing what they had been doing before being interrupted by the exit of the Warrior's Only Son from the household to his new life as a soldier. Soon the clamor and the conversations around her had returned to normal.

But the Warrior's Second Wife didn't care. She stood at the top of the stairs until the sun went down, until the lamps at each side of the front gate were lit, until everyone else had gone to bed. She stood at the top of the stairs until the darkness settled around her, accompanied by the evening dew. Her hair, tied at the back of her neck with a ribbon, grew damp and stuck to her face and neck; the fibers in the Chrysanthemum Kimono and its embroidery grew heavy and hung limply from her shoulders, the hem pooling around her shoes.

At last, when the horizon began to brighten with the rising sun, she withdrew to her room.

She vowed to stay there until her Son returned to her.

Or until she died.

****

It seemed as though the household forgot about her after that. Her Warrior Husband never called for her, and now that the Chrysanthemum Kimono was ruined, Her Warrior Husband's Other Wives lost interest in her. The Seamstress continued to bring her meals, however, and the Cat and the Chrysanthemum Kimono continued to be her companions. She sat in her room and embroidered, or stared out into her garden, the purring Cat on her lap.

Every year, the Warrior's Second Wife received a new kimono. It was the same with the other wives. Every one of them received at least one kimono, made of silk. Her Warrior Husband's more favored Wives received ones decorated by embroidery or skilled painters; some of his Wives received more than one.

But the Warrior's Second Wife only received one each year, usually pale or bland in color, and completely plain.

But, despite the glorious extravagance of color she had poured into the Chrysanthemum Kimono, she still had a wealth of threads remaining. Most of the brightest and richest colors had been used in the Chrysanthemum Kimono, of course...but she still had many colors left.

Each year, after receiving her new kimono, the Warrior's Second Wife and the Seamstress would sit together. The Warrior's Second Wife would draw the new kimono's design out on paper first, then together they would arrange and configure the design to the lines of the new kimono. The Warrior's Second Wife carefully planned each design to occupy her time until the next year's kimono arrived.

It was how she kept her sanity after the loss of her Son and the loneliness of being Her Warrior Husband's forgotten Wife.

****

Many years passed.

One year, the Warrior's Second Wife's new kimono was cut closer to her body; the sleeves were less long and full. She had not gained any weight; in fact, she was being brought a little less food each day by the Seamstress. She had actually lost some weight.

The year after that, the kimono was cut the same as the year before, but it was a hand's length shorter. The year after that, it was shorter still. And the Warrior's Second Wife noticed that meat had disappeared from the dishes the Seamstress brought her from the kitchen

"What is going on?" she asked the Seamstress one day when she brought her food. It was nothing but rice and some cooked cabbage.

"There are rumors your Warrior Husband is meeting defeat time and again on the battlefield," the Seamstress told her. "He has lost many soldiers. Many of the servants in the house now work in the fields; some of them fear he will call them away to be his soldiers soon."

"Many soldiers lost," the Warrior's Second Wife murmured to herself. She was silent a moment, then a fearful thought came to her. "Surely my Son is not lost?" she cried, afraid. Surely he was no longer a young boy now, but nearly thirteen.

The Seamstress took the Warrior's Second Wife's hands in her own; they had known one another by now for so long, this kind act in a moment of deep distress was permitted. "No, my Lady," the Seamstress said with a smile. "Everyone admires your Son greatly. He lives in the camp at the edge of the estate with the other soldiers, and he rides beside His Warrior Father when they go into battle, the two of them sitting straight and tall and absolutely fearless. They even say your Son is a better Warrior than his Father."

The Warrior's Second Wife sighed with relief. The Seamstress pushed the little bowl of rice and cabbage into her hands. "Eat," she encouraged her.

****

Although the days were lengthening in sunlight, an unseen darkness fell over the Warrior's household. Servants disappeared one by one: some of them to work in the fields; some to follow their Warrior Master into war; some simply died of old age or disease. The household became more and more silent.

The Seamstress even told her two of Her Warrior Husband's Newest and Youngest Wives had stolen away together in the middle of the night, using the darkness to hide their departure, returning home to their fathers. Naturally, leaving their husband and returning to their childhood homes was a disgrace, but it was better than starving to death.

Or, some whispered, it was better than facing rape and execution by the enemy when they invaded their Warrior Husband's estate and took all it contained as the spoils of war.

****

When it was time for the Warrior's Wives to receive the next year's kimono, they were found to be made of cotton, not silk. They were to dress as any common woman working in the fields.

The Warrior's Second Wife gave it little thought. It was a plain, white thing, nearly sheer it was so light. Her custom of embroidering her kimonos led her not to be critical of the unusual fabric, but rather she considered how she might embellish it. It was going to be difficult this year, as she had used nearly all her colorful threads and now was left with mostly shades of white at her disposal. Nevertheless, she was startled when her Warrior Husband's Fifth Wife threw her kimono on the floor and trampled it in disgust.

"It's an insult! I won't wear cotton; I deserve nothing less than silk!" she cried.

And she marched to her room, her face and neck and ears red in fury. She called for her servants to gather her things. By the evening she and her belongings - even some of the house furnishings that had been part of her dowry - were packed and on their way back to the village of her childhood. For the Warrior's Fifth Wife, the return home was not a matter of her own disgrace, but the disgrace of her Warrior Husband. For it was he who was losing the war and failing to provide her the life of a proper Warrior's Wife.

The household became even quieter after that. The Warrior's Second Wife embroidered her new, plain, white cotton kimono, but she had too little thread left, so the design was simple and she was able to finish it more quickly than usual.

She was bored after that and unable to sleep at night, so when the rest of the household slept, she wandered the corridors of the house. One night she ventured down the hall to the empty quarters of her Warrior Husband.

There were three rooms there. His room for sleeping; his room for the time spent with his wives, and his study. She reached her hand out to open the door of his wives' room, but withdrew her hand before she opened the door. No, too many things had happened in that room she would rather not consider, so she wouldn't enter. It represented loneliness and rejection to her. He called his other wives to himself more frequently in that room than he had ever called her, and the memory of so much rejection was too painful.

She turned to his sleeping room. She opened the door, her little lantern casting its brave light into the middle of the room, too feeble to reach into the far corners. She stared into the room a few moments, imagining what his nights had been here. To her surprise, she sensed a loneliness nearly as deep and despairing as her own, as if her Warrior Husband had gained as little from his wives and his wealth as she had gained from his love. Feeling as if she had intruded, she quickly withdrew and closed the door.

She turned to the library, his study.

Her Warrior Husband strictly forbid his wives or any of the female servants to enter. Knowing that, she opened the door without hesitation and with a sense of pleasure. She even wore a smile.

It was as if she had opened a door to a magical world.

The room was located on the side of the house that caught the full effect of the moon. The scrolls, the tables, the chairs all glowed with a silver light that drew her in. The room was masculine, full of sharp-edged but smooth wood, polished to a mirror-like finish, its angles punctuated with decorative planes of highly-polished brass. The room shifted and glowed like a jewel in the moonlight, the scrolls scattered about tempting her like fragrant flower petals floating in a glowing pond. These were scrolls, she knew, containing wisdom ranging from commerce to agriculture to warfare; knowledge typically thought to be too complex for a woman's feeble mind. But in the household of her father, such scrolls had been freely shared with her. In fact, her father had told her that this was one of her assets, that attracted her Warrior Husband to her; that led him to ask her father for her hand. Her father had even included some of his own priceless scrolls in her dowry. She carried the scrolls herself as she crossed the threshold into her Warrior Husband's home the day they married. He had welcomed her warmly, taking the scrolls from her and enfolding her in his arms, holding them both as if they were sacred objects and he was honored to be entrusted with them. She had thought when they were first married that her Warrior Husband might have taken her as his equal.

But after their first night together, he locked the scrolls away and never let her see them again.

She moved through the room now with her tiny lantern, looking for her father's scrolls. She finally found them, on a shelf by themselves, just at eye-level: a place of honor where her Warrior Husband must have frequently consulted them. She took one from the shelf, relishing the feel of it in her hands again, smiling at the warmth of her childhood memories of reading it again with her strong yet gentle father. She turned from the shelf so she could see the figures written there in the bright light of the moon.

Slowly, out of the darkness to one side of the door, the darkness began to take shape and solidify. Frozen, the scroll still in her hands, she watched, horrified, imagining evil was materializing out of the shadows. The figure grew taller and wider; it developed strength and depth.

But it was not just a vision - it carried the odor of wind and fear and death. She could smell the sweat of men and of horses; the odors of excrement and blood. She gripped the scroll, as if the knowledge and the memories it contained would give her strength.

The figure stepped into the moonlight.

It was her Warrior Husband.

He looked like a God of War, covered in the remains of battle and journey. He had not rested or eaten or bathed in days.

She waited for a roar of fury to come flying from him against her, for being in his private rooms and for handling his scrolls. As she waited, she stood before him, motionless with fear, the scroll still clutched in her hands.

He lifted his hands to the heavens in a gesture of utter despair. "I am so ashamed," he cried. "Our Son is lost!" And he fell to his knees, grasping at her feet. He lay on the floor before her, sobbing.

She was stunned. For a moment, she didn't move, didn't speak. She looked down at him, his stature collapsed, his dignity gone, clutching pitifully at the hem of her thin nightgown.

She pulled one foot back away from him. Then the other.

"Forgive me," he sobbed, crawling after her. "I failed. Forgive me."

It took all her strength to ask him. "Our Son is lost? How is he lost?"

"Dead," her Warrior Husband answered. She could barely understand him; his face was pressed into the mat at her feet. He spoke to the bamboo, not to her. "He was killed by the enemy in battle."

She threw the scroll into the darkness of the room and began to beat his head and shoulders, striking his dirty, matted hair, opening wounds that had barely begun to heal. "How could you let this happen?" she screamed at him. "You promised to protect him! You promised you would die for him, that you would give your life for him! If he is dead, you should be dead, too!"

Her Warrior Husband merely lay at her feet, weeping, not even lifting his hand to fend off her blows. He finally mercifully gave way to unconsciousness. She continued beating him until she was spent. Then, with a final cry of despair, she collapsed on top of him, worn out by her effort and her grief.

The household found them together on the floor the next morning, armor and nightgown entangled; his leather and metal mixed with her white linen and exquisite embroidery.

****

49

Her Warrior Husband was taken to bed and nursed by his remaining Wives while his Second Wife watched from the doorway, silent and severe. But he never regained his strength. Finally, one day as he lay in bed, his breathing labored, he reached out his hand to her. "Come to me," he asked her.

Stubbornly, she shook her head.

"Please," he begged.

"I am waiting for you to die," she said bitterly.

"And so it will come to pass," he promised. "But come to me. I need to tell you I've wronged you. I know that now."

His words softened her. She stepped towards him. He took her hand. She refused to offer him any warmth, however. He held her hand tenderly nonetheless.

"You," he said tenderly and with more than a little pride, "are the cleverest of my many Wives."

"Yes, I know," she said, her tone sarcastic. "*I* gave you a Son."

He closed his eyes briefly at her attack, but quickly opened them again. "I didn't mean that, although that was a great and wonderful Gift. No - of all my Wives, you are the one who can read and write. I have not appreciated you; I have not utilized your Knowledge and Wisdom. But now I must rely on it, if you will be so generous to share. The household will depend on you."

Her cheeks flushed unwillingly at his praise. "What can I do?" For a moment she softened, and allowed herself to look at him. He was smiling tenderly at her, as when they first married. She felt herself being drawn to him, just as she had in those early days.

He sensed her tender feelings, and he squeezed her hand. "You must prepare the household. I have been greedy and fought many years to expand my land; I have gone too far and spread my resources too thin. Lately I have lost many battles and angered many other Warriors. It has cost me my Son." He turned and looked out into the garden where a light snow was falling. "Not now, but soon, they will very likely come here and try to take my land in retribution. You must defend yourself and the household."

Her Warrior Husband was putting her in charge?

She pulled her hand away in horror.

"No," he said, reaching for her hand, fumbling a bit for it a moment before finding it again, "Don't think you can't do it. I know you can. I give you freedom to read everything in my study. I no longer forbid it. Everything there belongs to you now. And I give you full authority over the household and every living thing in it."

Her Warrior Husband's First Wife stood at the foot of the bed. The Warrior's Second Wife looked at her, as if she held the answer to some overwhelming question. But instead of answering her, or coming back with some jealous and spiteful retort, the older woman bowed her head, her arms outstretched at her hips, palms up in a posture of servility. "As you command," the older woman said, without a trace of sarcasm.

Their Warrior Husband smiled at his First Wife. "There - you see? In my absence, my First Wife is leader. But even she defers to you. It is destined. Go. Do what you must - fight or run. But I know you will decide with wisdom. You will be fair and just."

And later that night, he peacefully died.

****

The Warrior's Second Wife bundled herself up afterwards and went outside to the garden, walking the labyrinthine paths in the snow. The gardens were large and well-designed, with many interesting inlets

51

and niches. She walked very slowly, covering every inch of the outside of the house. She walked all night and did not sleep, her mind churning.

When she returned to her rooms that morning, she found them completely bare. All her clothes, all her threads, her bedding, even the little basket she had set aside for the Cat to sleep in were gone. Had the other wives taken all her things and destroyed them out of envy? Perhaps that would have been - once. But now there were only three of them left, and their Warrior Husband's First Wife had seemed sincere when she had bowed her head to her in obedience earlier. And the Other Wife was his youngest, and pregnant. She was very young, and now, very afraid. It was very unlikely any of them would have taken her things away.

So what had happened?

She heard soft footsteps behind her. She turned. It was the Seamstress, carrying a stack of neatly-folded linens. "Where are my things?" the Warrior's Second Wife asked her.

The Seamstress smiled at her. "Come with me," she said.

So the Warrior's Second Wife followed her into the hall and to the left, where soon they ended up at the rooms of her deceased Warrior Husband. Several servants, together with her Warrior Husband's remaining wives, were scrubbing and polishing every possible surface. The room, which had been a cluttered, stagnant sickroom a few hours before was now aired out: clean and fresh. She even saw the Cat's bed tucked in a corner that would get the majority of the day's sun.

They all stopped working when they saw her in the doorway. They turned to her and bowed.

And so she bowed in return, to thank them for all they had done for her.

****

She began to study the scrolls in her Warrior Husband's library Some had been in her own father's library; others were new to her. She regained the knowledge she thought she'd lost, and added more to what she knew.

It was currently winter. She had time, if she used it well, to gather information and to think. Armies rarely fought in winter; it was too difficult to move an army across great distances and keep men fed. An attack, if it came, likely wouldn't come until spring. And so, she decided the first thing she must do was to take stock of everything in the household - number of people, number of animals, how many weapons and farm utensils. But most importantly - how much food.

Fortunately, they had had a good harvest that year. Nevertheless, she ordered the food to be stored, to ensure it could last as long as possible. What could be preserved, she ordered preserved. And what could be dried, she ordered dried.

And then she implemented severe but fair rationing for everyone in the household. The amount of food each person received was based on their age, weight, and how much energy they expended in a day. Members of Her Warrior Husband's Family and his Third Wife were horrified, but their Warrior Husband's First Wife understood; their Warrior Husband's Second Wife was ensuring the remaining Warriors and those servants who worked in the fields were well-fed and enabled to keep up their strength. In reality, none of them were starving - yet.

And so, as the Warrior's Second Wife stood at the top of the stairs, announcing her plans to the household to try and save them all, the Warrior Husband's First Wife folded her hands within her kimono, standing quietly behind their Warrior Husband's Second Wife as she spoke, her solemn expression declaring her approval of the Second Wife's plans for them all. When necessary, she glared down any dissenters.

The Warrior's Second Wife did more, however. She interviewed each of her Warrior Husband's soldiers, seeking details of their last campaign, particularly regarding the condition of the Emperor's soldiers, their armor and weapons, and what direction they were headed when they left the battlefield.

However, her Warrior Husband's two remaining Commanders were too ill to meet with anyone; their wives were caring for them in their homes.

While she waited for them to recover, she organized her Warrior Husband's scrolls. They had been scattered around the room; the servants had merely gathered them up and straightened them. But the Warrior's Second Wife took them out again, making more of a mess than there had been before.

She discovered scrolls on warfare, on farming, and on history. All of these were written in the hands of the experts in each field. She clustered like subjects together.

Then she discovered several scrolls in her Warrior Husband's handwriting. They were his diaries, recording his personal life - such as the day he wed her, for example. But other scrolls were records of his battles - the strategy, the number of men, who had been wounded, and who had died.

Because his history so closely touched her own, she read them with great interest. He even wrote of the death of their Son, how her Warrior Husband and her son, eight at the time, had been surrounded by the enemy. Her Warrior Husband and several of his soldiers managed to fight well enough to get away, but the boy was dragged off his horse and pulled to the ground, where the enemy surrounded and overcame him. The last sight her Warrior Husband had of their Son was one hand lifted out toward him in a vain plea for help. But by that time, his Warrior Father and all his soldiers were running away, moving towards safer ground. To turn back and try to save him would have meant suicide. She wept as she read the descriptions, and felt the grief of her Warrior Husband through his words. He had never struck her as a man who was soft or who had any emotional feeling. Yet here were his words, thoughtfully chosen, bold and brutal and merciless in drawing the scene, unflinching in their gaze. But despite their boldness, there was a vulnerability in them, as if he had been writing through his tears. She wept that, after his return from war, she never allowed him to share in their mutual grief. Afterwards, she sat a moment, spent, sorting through his words in his mind, saving the best and most honorable of them for her heart's memory. When she felt she had had enough, she wiped away her tears and put the scroll away, carrying to a conspicuous shelf. She laid it there with great but simple care. It would be the only scroll to lie in that spot, in a place of honor.

She took a deep cleansing breath and turned to the remaining scrolls in her Warrior Husband's study.

She had much to read, and much to learn.

****

She read about farming and military tactics and strategy, diplomacy, and through her Warrior Husband's personal notes, much about the way his enemy fought and thought.

It would be unlikely that the Emperor would attack before spring; highly unlikely even that soon.

So, what was to be done?

She was overwhelmed; it turned into anger for herself. For all her reading, she felt she didn't know anything about military strategy, or how to wage a battle, or how to negotiate a surrender. How could she do this?

In the corner, the Cat woke briefly, stretched with a little grunt of pleasure, and curled up to go to sleep again. The Warrior's Second Wife smiled and shook her head. Animals! What did they know?

She turned back to her reading, but after a moment turned back to the Cat again. What wisdom could she find in a sleeping Cat? She studied the creature a moment. The cat was completely relaxed, curled into a soft, warm little oval, its tail curled around its body and tucked under its chin, its whiskers perfectly relaxed. She even appeared to be smiling, as if she were having a pleasant dream.

The Warrior's Second Wife gave a harsh, humorless little laugh. The Cat wouldn't sleep if it understood the frightening situation they were in. If the Cat knew the trouble they faced, she would be anxious, too, pacing the halls at night and twitching its tail with worry. If the Cat only knew…

And then something in the Warrior's Second Wife's mind shifted.

What if the Cat did know how dire their situation was?

What it the Cat knew and slept peacefully anyway?

What if the Cat knew nothing could be done in the middle of the night, and used that time to get good rest to rejuvenate her body, mind, and soul?

She got up from the desk and went to the Cat, scratching it ears. It lifted its face to her as if acknowledging her presence. It smiled at her, then tucked its head down over its tail again.

"All right, little Cat," the Warrior's Second Wife said. "Just for tonight I will follow your suggestion and sleep. I will see how I feel in the morning."

And so the Warrior's Second Wife went to her own bed, tried to clear her mind and relax her body. It took some doing, but after a short time, she fell into a deep and restful sleep.

****

The next morning she woke and asked the Cook to bring her breakfast - a meal she had often skipped to ensure others had her portion. But perhaps it would be better to keep up her own resources, rather than sacrificing herself for others. When she had finished her small but adequate breakfast, she dressed and went to her Warrior Husband's study to read more of his scrolls.

As she read, she suddenly found her mind was clearer. She remembered things she thought she had forgotten. She discovered greater insights, making connections, realizing, for example, that some foods lent themselves more favorably to drying, making them lightweight and therefore more practical for a warrior to carry on a long campaign.

At the end of the day, she felt she had learned much and didn't feel as overwhelmed as the day before.

The Cat was asleep on its bed again at the end of the day. The Warrior's Second Wife decided she would not stay up as late as she had been of late; she would go to bed and fall asleep again with lovely, peaceful thoughts. And so she did.

****

A plan was beginning to form in her mind. Through her reading, she was beginning to finally understand that she had to take into account all the assets of her household and analyze them with a view towards military tactics.

It was clear she did not have the means to summon an army. Too many men had been lost in earlier battles against the Emperor. And with their loss - either by death or having been taken prisoner - many of their wives had left their Warrior's household and returned to that of their parents', taking their children with them. So the population of the estate had dramatically decreased. And the majority of those remaining were women - the wives of the peasant workers.

Therefore, there was no possibility of launching an offensive against the emperor. She would have to focus on defense.

Fortunately, her Warrior Husband already took care of much of that by building his estate in rough mountain territory. The house stood high, with its back against the rock. The road reaching the estate was full of twists and turns and rocks. Someone on foot or on horseback could manage it well enough, but it would be nearly impossible for an entire army that didn't know the way.

Although the rough ground leading up the mountainside was difficult, the soil was healthy and rich. The Warrior's Second Wife researched carefully and decided that her first priority would be to plant crops - nutritious food well-suited to their soil, food that dried and kept well so her own few soldiers could transport it easily if needed.

She also decided to begin training the other women, no matter if they were well-born or peasant. But instead of telling them they were being trained to fight, she devised their training to appear more as a dance. She told them to dress in short but flowing robes, so that when they worked in formation in the courtyard, they spun and turned and jumped, looking like flowers blown in the wind. She kept her mood light while working with them; she wanted to gain their confidence and their trust, as there might be some day in the future when it would be necessary for them to follow her lead.

The women were pleased with the results of this work in their bodies. They were fitter and trimmer and had more energy.

And more than that, the petty fighting amongst them had begun to melt away. They were happier; their wits were sharper, and they all seemed to understand their unspoken yet required reliance on one another.

****

The Warrior's Second Wife had understood that although her Warrior Husband had never won his war against the Emperor, he had severely disabled him. She had heard it might take the Emperor some time to recover his forces, and she intended to use every week to her advantage.

But how? There was no way a group of women and a handful of men - most of them elderly or battle-scarred - could hold off the Emperor's armies.

The problem never left her thoughts. It plagued her sleep; when trying to read, she couldn't sit still. It was as if a wheel were turning on its own, constantly stirring her thoughts against her will, blowing her thoughts away like so many papers in a breeze.

The Warrior's Second Wife was pacing in her Warrior Husband's study one day, trying to decide which scroll she ought to read again for insight when the Seamstress came to her, bearing her embroidery basket and a bit of cloth.

The Warrior's Second Wife waved her away. "Not now. I haven't the time."

The Seamstress shook her head and extended the basket again. "No. You must take the time."

"No…"

"It will give your mind the break it needs," the Seamstress said kindly but firmly.

The Warrior's Second Wife stopped and looked at the Seamstress, this kind woman who had been such a steadfast friend for so many years. In her eyes, she saw love and concern, worry and compassion. The Warrior's Second Wife was touched by her loyalty. She nodded and took the basket, then settled in a corner where the light was especially good. She took up the cloth, threaded her needle and began to stitch. It only took a moment for her to be drawn in by the colors and the smooth feeling of drawing the silk thread through the fabric. Her shoulders relaxed; the line between her brows softened, and she began to lose herself in her work.

The Seamstress watched her a moment, then smiled. "I will bring you some tea," she said quietly, and left the room.

Alone, the Warrior's Second Wife allowed her thoughts to drift. She let the vibrant blues, pinks, purples, yellows and reds dazzle her eyes; the spaces between the motifs of her work drew her in; playing as they skipped over the fabric.

No - she pulled herself back to her problems. Work on the embroidery, but think about her tactics. What military move could she make against the Emperor when she had so few to fight, most of them women? What weapons could they use? What weapons did they have at their disposal? What could she rally against the Emperor?

She had run out of thread and needed to refill her needle. She reached into her basket for another length of blue thread, but realized she had finally used the last of the supply her Warrior Husband had given her. She was running out.

She looked at her work, disappointed. This wasn't what she had planned on. She had counted on finishing outlining that one flower in blue.

Well, disappointed or not - did she want to finish this piece or give up?

Finish, she decided. She stirred in her basket and found a length of purple, so jewel-like in tone it shimmered in her fingers. She smiled and threaded her needle.

A few stitches on, she stopped and examined her work. She actually realized she liked the effect of the purple better than the blue! Smiling, she continued to work.

Suddenly, it came to her. It was such a stunning thought, she sat up straight, a smile on her face clearer and more radiant than she had smiled in weeks.

Just then, the Seamstress returned with the tea. Seeing the

Warrior's Second Wife sitting up so straight, beaming, she was forced to ask, "Is everything all right?"

The Warrior's Second Wife smiled and nodded. "Come over here," she said to the Seamstress. She held up her embroidery as the other woman approached her. "What do you think?"

The Seamstress took the piece of fabric and examined it. She smiled. "I wouldn't have thought to put the blue and the purple together like that, but I like it. It's very pleasing." She giggled, then covered her mouth quickly, afraid the Warrior's Second Wife might think her disrespectful. "I'm sorry - I didn't mean to laugh. But I just thought that it feels like my eyes are being tickled. It's very pretty, but unexpected."

For a moment, the Warrior's Second Wife felt as if the world had stopped turning; that something of grave importance had been dropped in her lap. "What did you say?" she asked the Seamstress. "Say that again?"

"What?"

"What you just said - say it again."

"It's unexpected?"

"And that other thing you said…"

"What was that?"

"About your eyes…"

The Seamstress looked confused. "About my eyes being tickled? But that was so silly…"

The Warrior's Second Wife held out her hands to the Seamstress, her gesture asking that her work be returned to her. The Seamstress gave it to her, and the Warrior's Second Wife studied it with a concentration that seemed odd to the Seamstress. The Warrior's Second Wife had been working on the piece for several weeks now; it had been in her hands all afternoon just today. But now she was looking at it as if she had never seen it before. The Seamstress drew close to her. "What is it you see?" she asked quietly, expectantly.

The Warrior's Second Wife thought for a moment, looking first at her embroidery, then the needle in her hand, the length of thread still running through its eye. "I think I've learned something," she said, her tone laced with wonder.

The Seamstress waited for her to continue.

"First, I wasn't going to use this purple thread. But I had run out of the blue. But the purple was all I had. And it showed me: what you have is adequate. I also learned that what I have can be used in new and not only adequate, but perhaps even interesting ways..."

The Seamstress wasn't impressed. The Emperor and his armies were an imminent threat, and here the Warrior's Second Wife - the one who was now their leader - was going on and on about embroidery. "So?" the Seamstress said. But as soon as she said it, she regretted it. This time she did sound disrespectful.

But the Warrior's Second Wife didn't seem to mind. "Don't you see? It means we already have everything we need; we just have to be sure we use it wisely and carefully, and use it in new and interesting ways we may not have thought of before."

The Seamstress frowned at the Warrior's Second Wife. She understood her words, but was not sure what they might mean in practice. The Warrior's Second Wife saw the confused look on her face.

"Look, we can't strike first and attack the Emperor. I realize we do not have the forces to do that. But for the first time, I think we might be able to defend ourselves."

The Seamstress looked at her with a dubious expression.

"Yes. Yes, I believe we could," the Warrior's Second Wife said with conviction. "And even though I do believe we may not ultimately win, I believe we may be able to survive." She smiled at the Seamstress.

"Survive and *more*."

The Seamstress looked at her in disbelief. "And how could we do that?" she asked in disbelief.

The Warrior's Second Wife smiled. "Watch and see," she said.

****

The next day, the Warrior's Second Wife sat at her Warrior Husband's desk for many hours, staring out the window, studying scrolls concerning seasons and farming, and scribbling furiously on paper, bouncing between each activity with little rhyme or reason. Finally, she reduced all her notes into one scrap of paper and called the Seamstress to her.

"What do you hear of my Warrior Husband's Commanders?" she asked. "Are they recovering well?"

"One is doing better than the other," the Seamstress replied. "What is it you desire?"

"Ask them to come see me."

And so the two Commanders did. One was elderly and frail; he entered her Warrior Husband's study being carried by two men. The other Commander, a middle-aged man with graying temples, was in much better health. He entered with the use of a cane, but otherwise under his own power.

Both Commanders bowed to her.

The Warrior's Second Wife bowed in return.

"I think I can see the answer to my question already," she said. "I was going to ask how you are healing." She approached the Elder Commander, who was only half-sitting up on the litter on which he was carried. She held her hand out to him and he pressed his forehead to it in a gesture of respect. "I am sorry, Elder Commander," she said tenderly. "For the moment you must return to your bed and continue to heal." The Warrior's Second Wife turned to the younger man. "But you, Younger Commander, I have a mission for you."

And the mission was this: the Younger Commander would accompany the Eldest of her Warrior Husband's daughters to lands closer to the Emperor in an effort to learn if the Emperor had plans for retaliation against them. They would disguise themselves as father and daughter, craftsmen traveling to sell wares from their region.

They would pose as embroidery merchants.

The next morning the Younger Commander and the Warrior's Eldest Daughter set out with a horse and a cart. In the back of the cart was a trunk full of embroidery - ladies' kimonos, slippers for women and girls, embroidered scarves and sashes.

They traveled nearer and nearer to the regions of the Emperor, being careful to hold back of how much of their embroidery they sold along the way - they had to be certain they still had enough to sell when they entered the regions of the Emperor to be convincing.

Finally they reached an area only five miles from the Emperor's palace, where a fair was being held where all sorts of wares and foods were being offered for sale. They set up a table with the items in the trunk and waited for something to happen.

For a long time, nothing did. People passed by their table, stopped and looked at their wares a moment, then moved on. They sold one or two items, but nothing of any significance.

And then the atmosphere of the fair changed. Two young men had entered the grounds of the fair, their demeanor laced with arrogant swagger.

Their clothes were the colors of the Emperor's household.

The Younger Commander and the Warrior's Eldest Daughter exchanged a glance. This was why they had come! The two young men from the Emperor's household moved among the stalls and the tables, one of them fingering the merchandise as if he had a special appreciation for the work. The Warrior's Eldest Daughter took up a pair of embroidered slippers and held them out to the men, offering them a closer look.

"Pretty slippers?" she said with a charming smile. "For your women?"

One of the young men shoved her out of his way rudely. "No. We have no money for such luxuries," he said bitterly.

The Warrior's Eldest Daughter looked at them, indignant. "But you wear the robes of the Emperor's household! How is it you have no money?"

The shorter of the two young men looked at his friend, scowling at him as he pulled at his arm. "Don't say anything!" he warned, his voice low. "Who knows? They might be spies…"

But the taller of the young men shook his friend off as if he were nothing more than a tiny lapdog nipping at his heels. "These people are harmless," he said to his friend. He turned back to the Warrior's Eldest Daughter. "We don't have any money because the Emperor's coffers are currently depleted," he said. "The Emperor spread himself too thin during his last campaign. He lost a lot of men and supplies. Once we grow food again and our soldiers recover again and once -" and here the taller of the two young men turned and looked at his friend as if the two of them shared some secret knowledge, "- the Emperor learns better how to manage a military campaign, we will have money again for pretty little trinkets like yours."

The Younger Commander and the Warrior's Eldest Daughter bowed. Keeping perfectly in her role as an embroidery merchant, the Warrior's Eldest Daughter murmured, "And perhaps, sir, in that time my skills will be even more worthy of your coin."

The taller young man laughed at her and took her chin, tilting her face toward the sun. "Give us three years' time, my sweet. The Emperor will be ready for conquests again, and so will I."

His touch turned her stomach, but she smiled charmingly at him. As he and his friend walked away, the Warrior's Eldest Daughter and the Younger Commander heard the shorter young man say to his friend, "Why did you tell them three years? That could be critical information!"

"A tired, middle-aged man and his soft daughter whose head is full of thread and colors? They were no spies," the taller one said, waving the thought away as if it were a troublesome flea.

And the two young men from the Emperor's household melted into the crowd.

The Warrior's Eldest Daughter and the Younger Commander stared at one another, not believing their luck. "Do you think they might have been lying to us?" the Warrior's Eldest Daughter asked.

The Younger Commander shook his head. "I don't think so. I know that type of young man. They often think or act before they speak. They are foolish and quick to speak or act without thinking. Such men are often the first killed."

They said nothing more to one another, but stayed at the market, only taking down their table when the others did as well. But that night, while the city was still dark, they took up their wares, and quietly but swiftly headed home.

****

They arrived back at the Warrior's household and immediately went to see the Warrior's Second Wife. But before she let them speak, she called for the Elder Commander, so they all could hear the report of the Younger Commander and the Warrior's Eldest Daughter. Together, they listened quietly, then sat in silence, pondering.

"Do you think it's true?" the Warrior's Second Wife asked the Two Commanders.

"Yes," the Elder Commander replied. "Our last battle against the Emperor was long and difficult, but he didn't have the forces to come back and take our Warrior's Estate. The Emperor's men were tired and hungry. That means not only was his army low on food, but so is his entire kingdom."

The Younger Commander nodded in agreement. "The Emperor will need to rebuild not only his army but also his resources. And that means he needs time to grow and harvest food. Three years would be a reasonable estimate."

The Warrior's Second Wife was silent several moments, thinking. "Is it possible," she finally said, "that we could expect it will be three years, then, before the Emperor might come to take our estate?"

The Two Commanders exchanged a look, wordlessly consulting one another's experience and expertise. Finally, the Elder Commander nodded. The Younger Commander spoke.

"Yes. Based on what we ourselves saw the last time we encountered the Emperor, and what we heard, you can easily count on three years."

The Warrior's Second Wife took a deep breath to steel herself for the next question. "Would either of you recommend that we consider attacking the Emperor while he is weak? Go for the first strike?"

Again, the Two Commanders exchanged a look. "No," the Younger Commander said after a moment. "Even as weak as he is, the Emperor is still stronger than we are. It would be foolish for us to attack him. But the journey from where he sits on the throne is too far for his troops in their weakened condition. He will come for us. But it will take him three years to recover and prepare."

The Warrior's Second Wife saw the terror rise in her Warrior Husband's First Wife's eyes. Yes, it was terrible to think that they might only have three years before the Emperor came for them.

But they had three years. With luck, perhaps a little more.

The Warrior's Second Wife drew herself up, straightening her spine in determination. "Then if offense is not an option, we must plan our defense instead," she said.

"So what is your plan?" the Elder Commanders asked her.

She turned to him, her answer as sure and confident as a schoolgirl who has spent days and weeks studying and preparing well for a final examination. "Build our strength, focus on building our defense tactics, and when confronted, defend ourselves with keen strategy."

The Elder Commander smiled at her and nodded. "Well done," he said.

But the Warrior's Second Wife had one more defense in mind when her other two tactics failed - as they inevitably would against the Emperor's superior strength. But this one was her secret alone, until the time was right.

****

The Warrior's Second Wife began by planting crops - food that grew well in the soil surrounding their household, food that was hearty and healthy to eat; delicious food that could be dried or otherwise preserved. She ordered that the mandatory military training for everyone on the estate be upgraded. Strength was vital, but knowing how to follow orders and work as a team was also important. It was important to the Warrior's Second Wife that the souls of the people she was responsible for were well-fed, too. In their spare time, they worked stitching or sewing or reading or writing or doing any other of a myriad of crafts.

During these times, it was as if a peace settled over the household, and with it a golden light and the soft tinkling of delicate silver bells that were soothing to the eye and ear…

****

A year later, the Warrior's Second Wife sent the Younger Commander and her Warrior Husband's Eldest Daughter out to pose as merchants again. When they returned, they told stories of how the Emperor's lands were greener, his people a little plumper, but the soldiers wandering among the people in the market still appeared tired and drawn.

This was good news. The Emperor would probably rest another year. But the Warrior's Second Wife knew she had to remain true to her plans, and maintain a tight discipline in her household.

Her Warrior Husband's estate consisted of a hill topped by his magnificent house for his own wives and children. The sides of the hill were dotted with fields and the homes of his workers and soldiers. It all was as tempting to an enemy as a tree heavy with ripened fruit.

The Warrior's Second Wife went out one day to study the estate of her Warrior Husband. The Two Commanders went with her. They rode together on their horses silently. The Two Commanders had come to respect the Warrior's Second Wife as nearly their equal in intellect, so they waited for her to speak first. They circled the entire base of the hill, a journey that took them from dawn until late afternoon. When the Warrior's Second Wife stopped, they stopped, and she studied the side of the hill, although neither of the Commanders understood why. For a long time, she was silent. After a few moments, she would move on again for a while, then stop again.

At the end of the day, they returned to the house at the top of the hill. The Two Commanders tried to follow the Warrior's Second Wife when she walked to her Warrior Husband's study, but she stopped at the door and turned to them. "No, please. Not tonight. Tomorrow. I promise to meet with you tomorrow." And she entered her Warrior Husband's study and closed the door, locking them out.

The Warrior's Second Wife sat up all night, squinting in the dim light of a single lantern, too immersed in thought to light more, drawing the hill from five sides, pinpointing particular areas, analyzing, thinking, then drawing some more. The Two Commanders stayed outside her door, taking turns to nap briefly. But the next morning, when she opened the door, they were both wide awake and waiting for her.

She didn't seem at all surprised to find them in the hall. "Come in," she said, opening the doors wide.

She led them to the desk and the drawings she had of the mountain. "I have an idea," she said.

The three of them leaned over her drawings. "I believe we are strongest here." And the Warrior's Second Wife pointed to seven areas she had found from her tour of the estate the day before.

The Two Commanders considered her analysis seriously, then nodded gravely in agreement.

The Warrior's Second Wife indicated four other areas of her drawings. "And weakest here."

Again, after a moment's thought, the Two Commanders agreed.

The Warrior's Second Wife smiled. "I have a plan."

****

They began by making the most vulnerable areas appear to be unattractive and treacherous as possible. Using paper and glue, they created realistic-looking boulders, painting them to look craggy and rough, then lacquered them to withstand the elements. They then stacked these boulder creations in natural-looking formations, anchoring them to the ground so that neither wind nor rain would dislodge them. They then built shelters that dissolved into the surroundings and stocked them with hundreds of lanterns and the means to light them all. They reinforced the area with walls and spikes buried into the ground, making it difficult for an enemy to ascend the hill.

As for the areas that were already naturally strong, they also built walls and spikes that would make it difficult to scale the hills, but they disguised them to blend in with the terrain, making them invisible. They landscaped the area with a variety of beautiful blossoming trees and shrubs - inviting for an intruder, but providing excellent coverage for a defender of the Warrior's estate who would be lying in wait.

And how it all worked out was this:

A year or so later, when the Emperor's troops had recovered a bit of their strength, they began moving towards the estate of the Warrior who had so weakened them. They found it set upon a mountain, with areas that appeared soft and easy to climb, but with other areas of rougher terrain. As the Emperor's scouts studied the mountain, they saw fires - many fires that undoubtedly meant a large amount of the Warrior's soldiers were huddled over to stay warm and heat their evening meals - men that were lying in wait for them. They decided to avoid those areas and find another way to conquer the mountain.

What the Emperor's soldiers didn't realize, however, was that the fires were only many lanterns, not many men. In reality, only ten or fifteen people were actually there, but each person had lit a hundred or more lanterns.

And when the Emperor's forces tried to take the pathways that looked so promising and accessible, they were thwarted by barriers painted to look like pleasant trees and shrubbery and grasses. The men and their horses were defeated by obstacles of all sorts that barred their way or sent them further out of their way than desired.

The Emperor's soldiers fell back from these advances; they also lost a number of soldiers and horses. But a few days later, they would try again. Although their numbers dwindled, they continued to make slow and steady progress up the mountain, getting a little closer to the main household of the estate every day.

It became clear that although the plan of the Warrior's Second Wife had bought them time, it would not ultimately save them.

The Two Commanders were concerned. For several days they did not mention this to the Warrior's Second Wife. But finally their concerns outgrew their ability to keep silent and they, together with the Warrior's First Wife, went to see her.

They spoke first of the success of her plan in stifling the efforts of the Emperor's army to reach and claim the estate, but later shifted to their concerns that their tactics against the Emperor's forces were weakening and would soon collapse.

But the Warrior's Second Wife seemed neither surprised nor alarmed, or even offended that they were now questioning her. "How many men were there when they began their campaign up the mountain?" she asked.

"Nearly a thousand," the Elder Commander answered.

"And how many now?"

The Two Commanders looked at one another, silently trying to agree between themselves on a number. "Perhaps one hundred and fifty?" the Younger Commander guessed. The Elder Commander bowed his head in silent agreement.

"And how do the Emperor's men look?"

"Weary. Dirty. Hungry," the Elder Commander answered.

"And how many days, do you think, before they break through our walls?" the Warrior's Second Wife asked.

"Three or four days."

The Warrior's Second Wife smiled. "Then that is how long we have to work."

And she gave orders to prepare the most lavish of dishes, to clean the household from top to bottom - and all the people and animals within it. The gardens were weeded and groomed, and fresh flowers were cut and arranged in every conceivable corner.

She ordered everyone to dress in their best clothes.

And on the fourth day, the air heavy with the aroma of good food and fragrant flowers, everyone took their places in shimmering silks and brilliant embroideries.

And they waited, the Warrior's Second Wife at the top of the courtyard steps, opposite the great entry door. She wore her Chrysanthemum Kimono one arm shockingly bare, a figure both defiant and resilient.

It was as if the entire household formed a beautiful, living, powerful tableau of wealth and prosperity. If their boundaries were to be broken, they would proudly present the Emperor with all the glory of what he had just attained - and perhaps win his respect.

So when the handful of soldiers of the Emperor's army, thin and hungry as they were, entered the courtyard of the defeated Warrior, they saw the household of their enemy ready to greet them as if they were long-anticipated honored guests, each one of them impeccably groomed, unafraid, confident, and seemingly bursting with health, wealth, and prosperity. The utter silence of the household - broken only by the gentle notes of wind chimes here and there clashing with the clanking of their own swords and armor - was more powerful and threatening than the war cries of five hundred men.

And high above them, at the top of the steps, stood a woman wearing a Chrysanthemum Kimono, as if she were challenging the throne of the Emperor himself.

The three officers leading the remnant of the Emperor's army held up their hands, stopping the soldiers behind them from pressing forward. For a moment, they didn't know what to do, and whispered among themselves, trying to settle on a course of action. Should they slaughter them all? But they had not offered any resistance...Yet the soldiers were so hungry, and the food smelled so good...it would be so easy to drop at one of the tables laden with luscious food. Yes, perhaps it was a trick, but they were so hungry...

As they debated, no one - not a member of the Warrior's household, not a member of the Emperor's tattered troops - dared to breathe. Except for one of the Emperor's young soldiers. Despite his youth, he was rapidly proving himself to be a brilliant leader, once he became a little more seasoned on the battlefield. He had once been a portion of the spoils of war from some earlier campaign who had been left for dead by his members of his own army. No one - not even the Young Warrior - could remember where he had originally come from. All he could remember was that all his life he had been trained to be a soldier, and now his loyalty belonged to the Emperor.

But something had been odd as they had struggled to climb the mountain of their Warrior Enemy. It was as if pictures of long-forgotten dreams - dirty and faded with time - were being overlaid with new and fresher versions of the same scenes. He felt as if he had been here before - but that also perhaps he had not.

But when he entered the gates to the Warrior Enemy's household, and saw the Woman in the Chrysanthemum Kimono at the top of the stairs, one sleeve missing, a familiar white and orange Cat at her feet, the film slowly fell from his memories.

And he dropped his shield and his sword. They clattered to the ground, breaking the silence. He reached into his armor, past his jacket, past his shirt, to the piece of fabric he kept close to his heart, a sacred relic he somehow knew had been a part of his mother once. After a moment, he produced a piece of dark fabric, stained with the blood and dust and grit of a hundred battles, but still brilliantly embroidered with chrysanthemums in the same style and in the same hand as those on the robes of the woman at the top of the stairs.

The Young Warrior stepped in front of the Emperor's Three Commanders, the piece of fabric in his hand, holding it between the Commanders and the woman, so the connection between the fabric he held and the Kimono the woman wore was unmistakable. "Let there be no talk of violence here. Yes, these people are our enemies..." And he turned to the woman at the top of the stairs. "But this woman is my Mother. And I am finally Home."

The Young Warrior turned and walked up the stairs as the Warrior's Second Wife walked down. As they met in the middle, they embraced for a long time, the silence and the fragrance of a million flowers enveloping them.

****

Naturally, the Warrior's Household - all the land, the treasures, the scrolls, the crops and the people - became the property of the Emperor to be dispensed with as he saw fit.

But the Son of his Enemy - the child of the Warrior and his Second Wife - had served the Emperor so bravely and so loyally - he was made one of the Emperor's Commanders and was given leadership over 100,000 men.

And for his training camp, used to house and train the men, the Emperor gave him the Estate of his Warrior Father.

As for his mother, the Warrior's Second Wife, she was given the place of Honored Advisor in the Emperor's Court. For she had remained strong against the Emperor for a hundred days, raising neither blade nor arrow against the Emperor's Army, and had shown extraordinary courage, standing before the Emperor armed with nothing but a Chrysanthemum Kimono and a little white and orange Cat.

ABOUT THE AUTHOR

Elaine D.K. Hargrove is a graduate of the University of Minnesota and lives and works in Minneapolis. This is her first published work.